MORE THAN ANGER

LEXI BRUCE

An imprint of Enslow Publishing

WEST **44** BOOKS™

Please visit our website, www.west44books.com.
For a free color catalog of all our high-quality books,
call toll free 1-800-542-2595 or fax 1-877-542-2596.

Cataloging-in-Publication Data

Names: Bruce, Lexi.
Title: More than anger / Lexi Bruce.
Description: New York : West 44, 2020. | Series: West 44 YA verse
Identifiers: ISBN 9781538382639 (pbk.) | ISBN 9781538382646
  (library bound) | ISBN 9781538383322 (ebook)
Subjects: LCSH: Children's poetry, American. | Children's poetry,
  English. | English poetry.
Classification: LCC PS586.3 B783 2020 | DDC 811'.60809282--dc23

First Edition

Published in 2020 by
Enslow Publishing LLC
101 West 23rd Street, Suite #240
New York, NY 10011

Copyright © 2020 Enslow Publishing LLC

Editor: Caitie McAneney
Designer: Seth Hughes

Photo credits: cover (thread) xpixel/Shutterstock.com; cover (spark)
© istockphoto.com/dzika_mrowka.

Printed in the United States of America

CPSIA compliance information: Batch #CS18W44: For further information contact
Enslow Publishing LLC, New York, New York at 1-800-542-2595.

To the teachers who believed in me when I didn't believe in myself. You taught me to read, to write, and to persevere. You taught me how to turn my dreams into reality. Thank you.

FAMILY TIME

Anna, get off your phone,
Mom says.
It's time for dinner.
Dad's home. We're going out.

I sigh, text Jess, my best friend,
that we'll talk later.

I want to hear all about her new
boyfriend, Sam.
But for now it's family time.
Strictly enforced—
three dinners a week.

Even if it's only
a chance for them
to show the world

what a mess

we are as a family.

It's not like when I was little.

We'd go out for burgers together

just for the fun of it.

Dad would tell bad jokes

that he got out of a book.

But we'd laugh and laugh,

mostly because he was already

laughing so hard

he couldn't get the punchline out.

Now Dad talks about work

the whole ride over.

About how this idiot

screwed that up.

And the other idiot

did this wrong.

I tune him out.

I stare out the window,

people watching.

We seat ourselves

in a booth at the diner,

and then

they turn on me.

How's school?

Mom asks.

It's fine,

I say.

How'd that paper go?

Dad asks before I can

finish what I'm saying.

It was fine. Got a B-minus.

A B-minus!?

He almost shouts,
You can do better than that.

Would you stop picking on her?
Mom says,
B-minus is still pretty good.

What, you think she shouldn't
try to do better?
She's 16! She needs to
start acting like it.
You want her to grow up
to be stupid? Jobless?
He spits the words out
like he's disgusted.

What did you just say
to me?

Mom slams her menu
down on the table.
She lost her job a year ago.

We haven't even ordered yet
and they're already
causing a scene.

I glance around the diner
to make sure no one I know
can see this happening.

Mom, I'm sure he didn't mean it,
I say, but too quietly.
Neither of them notice me.

*Dad, I'll do better on
the next paper,*
I swear.

I speak a little louder,
and this time they hear me.

They glare at each other.
Then turn back to me.

So, Jess's mom said
there's a dance coming up.
Are you planning on going?

Mom asks, as if Dad hadn't
just called us stupid.
The question makes me nervous.
Because I think Dave is about to
ask me to that dance.

Yeah, I'm definitely going.
Can we go
dress shopping?

Mom starts to say yes,
before Dad
butts in.

No, she's not going!
She needs to
get her grades up.

My heart sinks.
This dance is my chance
to get to know Dave better.

We've sat next to each other
in third-period history
all year. We're always flirting
and joking before class.

Last week he did a dead-on
imitation of our teacher
that had me laughing
for the entire 42-minute period.

Anna is going to that dance
if I have anything to say about it,
Mom says,

just to spite Dad.

Dad's about to respond
when I change the subject
just to spare us all that argument.

Hey, where are we going
on vacation this summer?

We talk about
Cape Cod, Orlando,
San Francisco, or Yellowstone.

We spend the rest of dinner
discussing where we really
want to be, ignoring the tension.

I imagine myself, alone.

Exploring a jungle somewhere.

Or hiking the Alps.

Any adventure that gets me

away from my parents.

THAT NIGHT

After dinner, we go home.

I go into the living room

to work on my

math homework.

If I pull my grades up,

Dad will let me go

to the dance.

I know I should

try harder anyway,

if I want to go to a good college

and become a journalist

and travel the world,

reporting stories

that change history.

I plop down on the couch,
pull the quilt off the back,
and wrap it around me.

I flip open my book
and wonder why I'll need to know
how to find the area of a triangle
if I'm reporting on world events.

I sigh and start figuring
out the first homework problem.

Dad's sitting in the living room, too.
He's squinting at his laptop.
No doubt some important work thing.

He works for the government.
He studies the spread of disease
and figures out how to stop it.

He's always working.
Always reading reports
and correcting mistakes.
Or he's off at conferences
or helping out in other cities.

Mom's on a cleaning spree
right now.

She's been doing that
a lot since she lost her job
as a kindergarten teacher
last year.

Now she's home all the time
and the fighting is worse.
When they used to argue,
one of them would drop it
before it got out of hand.

Now when Mom's angry,
she won't let anything go.

Now she has time to stew
and get really ticked off about
the little things.

She yells more, so he works more.
Then she yells about that,
and then they start all over.

I hear her going down
to the basement to put in
a load of laundry.
She slams the washer lid shut.

When she comes back up,
I hear her pull the vacuum
cleaner out of the closet.

I grit my teeth as she
starts to vacuum the stairs.

I can't pay attention
to my homework with the noise.
But if I complain,
she'll start yelling at me
for not cleaning.

Dad's also getting mad
about the noise.
He's fidgeting
and he rolls his eyes.

Finally he slams
his laptop shut
and stands up
and storms upstairs.

Do you have to make
all that noise while
I'm trying to work?

His yelling is muffled
by the sound of the vacuum.

Hey, I'm trying to talk
to you.

The vacuum cleaner
turns off suddenly.
I know he's pulled
the plug out of the wall.

Yeah,
I hear you talking,
she snaps.

And maybe if I weren't busy
cleaning the whole house
by myself I might care.

I hear them stomping toward
the stairs.

Are you calling me lazy?
he snaps.

No, I'm calling you
a workaholic.
If you spent
any more time at work
you'd have to pay rent there!

I don't know how they expect me
to do well in school
if they're always yelling
when I'm trying to figure out
my math homework.

I snap my textbook shut,

grab my sneakers

and backpack,

and head out the door.

I'm not sure where I'm going.

But I'm not gonna

hang around the house

and listen to them fight all night.

I end up at the movie theater,

just in time to catch

the last show of the night.

It's one of those romantic

comedies where everyone's

a mess, but everything works out

anyway.

I wish real life were like that.

I wish I knew

that in the end

I'd get the cute guy from school,

the career as a traveling journalist,

and the dream house

in the country.

Far

away

from

here.

MATH CLASS

Monday I hand in my half-
done geometry homework.
The teacher hands back
last week's pop quiz.

I only got three out of eight questions right.

I remember working on
homework the night before the quiz.

I also remember being distracted. Because
Dad got home late from work.
And Mom started yelling at him.
And he called her a miserable woman.

I remember taking the quiz,
and as I looked at each question

all the formulas left my head

and all I could think of

were the insults my parents

had yelled.

Workaholic $\neq$ (miserable woman + drunk) x failure

As we go over the answers in class,

I see where I made my mistakes.

I wonder if

I would've made them

if I hadn't been distracted

by the yelling and swearing.

I wonder if they even realize

how distracting it is

to be so worried

that you can't think straight.

THAT KINDA GIRL

Jess says I should be more confident.

She says I should
just ask Dave
to the dance myself.
Because it's not the 1950s anymore,
she says.

I tell her,
I'm not pretty
enough, and anyway
I'm not that kinda girl.

You are so
pretty enough.
And you should learn to
be that kinda girl,

she tells me.
No one ever got
what they wanted
by being shy about it.

I don't tell her that I'm afraid
that if I become that kinda girl,
I'll fall in love with someone
and then come to hate them.

I don't tell her that
as much as I want someone
to love me, I can't get past
the fact that I've seen love
turn to hate so quickly.

LATER

I don't have to

be that kinda girl,

because Dave finds me

the next day,

between geometry and gym.

And he blushes and

mumbles. And asks me out.

And I say,

Yeah, sure, I guess.

I want to smile,

and I want him to know

that I like him

a lot. But I can't

get myself to say that.

It's just too risky.

We decide to get coffee together
on Saturday.

I'm smiling the rest of the day
because he's cute, and kind,
and smart.

And maybe I am enough.
And maybe I can be brave
and let him in.

And maybe one day
I *will* be
that kinda girl.

GETTING READY

Saturday comes and
I don't know if I'm
more nervous or excited.

I've never been on any
kind of date before.
I'm not sure
if I should dress up
or go casual.

I mean, it's just coffee.
But also he's *so* cute.

And thinking about him
makes me break into a smile.

I finally decide on my favorite
jeans, and a T-shirt that
brings out the green in my eyes.

I let my dark curls fall down
around my shoulders.
I brush a little mascara
onto my lashes.

And I actually
kinda like the way I look.
I feel more confident
than I think I've ever felt.

Dad's still mad
about my grades.
So I sneak out of the house
quietly, hoping he doesn't notice.

COFFEE

I meet Dave at the coffee shop

around the corner

from my house.

He smiles when I walk in.

We start off

with some awkward

small talk about school.

Then we find out

that we both like riding bikes

in a serious way.

I tell him that I've always

wanted to go on a trip,

riding my bike across the country.

He lights up,
and tells me that
sounds like a lot of fun.

Hey, maybe we should
do some bike rides
around the area this summer,
he says.
And then maybe
next summer we can do
something bigger,
go farther away.

Farther away is all I want.

We start planning
where we might go.
He pulls out his phone,
and we look online
for cool bicycle routes.

We laugh a lot,

and talk about music,

and how maybe we'll go

see Drake when he plays

in town over the summer.

And then suddenly it's hours later.

He has to get home

for his grandparents'

60th wedding anniversary.

I wish we could stay here

and keep talking

until the shop closes,

because it's just so easy

to talk to him. And when

he's around it's hard to be

sad or scared.

I still don't know how

to trust my heart.

But I stopped worrying

for a couple hours

and that's something at least.

I go home, happier

than I've been in a long time.

THE LETDOWN

All the way up the street
and to my front door
I think about how well
Dave and I get along.

I think about the way
his dark hair sweeps
across his forehead.

And the little dimple he gets
when he smiles.

I think about his dark brown eyes.
How he looks me straight in the eyes
when I talk. And I feel
like he actually cares about
what I have to say.

31

And then I open
the door to the house,
and I forget all of that.

I hear shouting upstairs,
and I tense up.
I walk into the house,
and see that the living room
is a disaster.

The coffee table is flipped
over. The stuff that
was on it is scattered
all over the floor.
There's a can of Pepsi spilled
onto the white carpet.

I hear them coming downstairs.

Before I can say anything,

Dad is out the door,

briefcase in hand.

Mom slams the door

shut behind him.

She lets out an

angry, wordless screech.

She turns around,

leans against the door.

Sinks down

until she's sitting on the floor.

She puts her head in her hands

and sits motionless,

her salt-and-pepper curls

falling over her eyes.

I go over to her, and put my arm
around her.

She looks up, surprised to see me,
and then buries her head
in my shoulder.

My mind is suddenly filled
with images of me and Dave
fighting like this
in another 20 years.

When he learns my flaws,
knows how bad my grades are,
or how moody I am,
I'm sure he'll hate me
as much as my parents
hate each other.

PLANNING

We sit there for awhile,
until she's breathing normally
again. And then I get up
and start making some
instant mac and cheese.

Mom and I are sitting
at the kitchen table and talking
about summer vacation
when Dad walks back in
hours later.

He joins us, and everyone pretends
that no one was shouting
and swearing
just a short time ago.

We're leaving the day after
my last final.

Now we're deciding
where to go.

Last year we
went to Maine.
We hung out
in a beach town
for two weeks straight.

Mom and I
laid in the sun,
and swam,
and took surfing lessons.

And pretended she hadn't just
lost her job after she stumbled in late
and hungover one morning.

Dad hung out on the beach,
but he never looked up
from his phone.

Important work stuff,
couldn't wait.

Because in all the offices,
he's the only one
who can fix the problem.
Whatever that problem is,
he never tells us.

This year, Mom's decided
we're going camping.
For a week. In a cabin.
In a state park in Vermont.

Dad's worried
he won't have cell service.

Mom acts

like she hadn't

even thought of that.

I'm just hoping we can all

survive each other.

BEDTIME

I'm curled up in bed,
covered in three blankets.
I'm trying to drift off,
but Mom's voice is angry downstairs.

Now that I'm out of sight,
they're back to fighting.

Do you ever listen to me?
she yells.
I told you to clean the drain
out last week,
and now it's clogged!
You're useless.

Dad says something
I can't hear.

Down in the the kitchen.

a pan slams on the counter,

and jolts me wide awake.

They forget that

sound carries.

They forget that

there's more

in this house

than their anger.

Sometimes I forget, too.

I forget that we used to laugh.

I forget being a family,

and enjoying dinnertime

together.

I forget what happiness
feels like.

I try to think about Dave
and how I felt with him.
But I can't focus on anything
other than the anger downstairs.
And the fear I feel curling
around my throat.

WHY!?

Why do you guys do this?

I want to scream at them.

Not just to each other. To me!

When they yell
and storm around and slam doors,
I'm invisible and muted.
And might as well
not be there at all.

And then I think something I've
never let myself think.

Why don't you just break up?

I wrap my fingers
around my pillow,
white-knuckled.
I fight the urge
to run downstairs
and say it to their faces.

I'm afraid of what
will happen if I ever
speak these things
out loud.

I'm sure it makes me
a terrible daughter
to wish these things.

But I don't know
how many more fights
I can stand to hear.

ANYWHERE BUT HERE

Bedroom door slams
shut. Angry silence
rings through the house.

They're asleep,
and now I'm free.
I peek out of my room
to see the hallway deserted.

I grab my sneakers and backpack,
creep down the stairs,
and out the back.

I pull my bike
out of the shed.

What I didn't tell Dave is that

the reason I like my bike

is that it gets me away from here.

I couldn't tell him that.

Or he'd know how messed up I am.

In the street,

I pull out my phone,

and dial Jess.

Hey, can I come by?

      Yeah, of course.

      You okay?

Yeah, I'm fine. Just bored,

I lie.

      Okay, see you in a few.

I send off a quick
text to my mom
so she won't panic
when she wakes up
and I'm not at home.

The street is so peaceful
at this time of night.

No yelling, no traffic, no people.

I breathe deeply
for the first time in hours.

I pedal to the park.
Ride
a few laps around
just for the
freedom of it.

Then I head
over to Jess's
to watch trash TV, eat junk food,
and not talk about what's
bothering me.

I think Jess knows
something's up,
but she knows better
than to ask.

Instead, she starts babbling
excitedly about Sam,
her new boyfriend.

It's just what I need
to take my mind off my parents.
I even fake a smile.

DRESS SHOPPING

I sleep over at Jess's

that night.

We go dress shopping

with her mom

the next morning.

Even though Dad's

still saying I can't go to the dance,

I know Mom will make sure I can.

We go to the mall

and try on so many

dresses.

And I hate the styles this year.

Empire waists

and too much fluff.

But I find the perfect one.

Emerald green, off the shoulder.

The shape fits my curves just right.

It's even in my price range.

I imagine myself wearing it,

Dave's hands on my waist.

And then I quickly push

that idea out of my head.

I'm getting attached already,

and that scares me.

FAMILY DINNER

After the mall,
we go back
to Jess's for dinner.

Dinner with her family
is warm and bubbly.

Her dad cooked
while we were out.

There's lasagna,
and salad, and vegetable soup.
It's all so delicious.

Her parents ask her about school.
They even let her talk
before they respond.

And they're excited for her

when she tells them

she got a B on a paper.

And when they ask

about her date to the dance,

they're eager to hear all

about the boy she's taking.

She gushes over Sam,

and how cute he is,

and how he's so funny.

Her little sister makes a face,

because boys are still icky.

Everyone laughs,

because we remember

Jess making the same face

when she was eight.

A BETTER WEEK

Monday starts off rough
because I get my geometry
homework back, and it's not great.

But then in biology I get a test
back. It's an A-minus.
I know Dad
will be satisfied with that.

Maybe it will put both of them
in a better mood. Maybe
they'll get along tonight.

When I get home, he's not
back from work yet.
I show Mom, and she smiles.

I leave the graded paper

on the kitchen table

so Dad will see it

as soon as he comes in.

He always grabs

an apple off the table

to have as a snack

when he gets home from work.

It's almost nine when he gets home,

and his shoulders are slumped.

He perks up when he sees

the grade. And for the first time

in a long time I feel like

I've actually done something right.

MAKEUP

Jess and I are dressing and doing

makeup at my house

before the dance on Friday.

I didn't want to have her over.

But when she asked,

I couldn't come up with

an excuse why not.

Our dates will pick us

up from here.

Then we'll go dance

the night away.

Up in my room, Jess brushes on

blush and applies eyeliner that's too thick.

Downstairs I hear thunder rumble

as Mom sees that

Dad's not home

from work yet.

He promised

to be home to see me

off to the dance.

He was so excited about

my biology test.

He said he hoped

I'd do as well on my finals.

He said I could go to the dance

as a reward.

Now Mom's stomping and storming

and cleaning in the loudest

way possible.

Your mom really likes to clean these days,
doesn't she?
Jess jokes, not knowing the difference
between just cleaning
and angry cleaning.

Yeah, you know her...
I respond, jokingly,
even though she doesn't know
Mom, not anymore.
She's a bit of a neat freak.

THE CALM

Dad strolls through
the front door just as
Jess and I are coming
down the stairs,
all dolled up and ready to go.

I freeze for a moment
because I know
Mom is mad and
Dad isn't prepared
for her anger.

Dad smiles at me
as he puts his briefcase
down by the door
and wraps me in a hug.

You look wonderful,

honey,

he says to me.

Ready for the big dance?

I twirl so that my skirt

flows out around me.

For a moment

I feel like a princess.

Like tonight can be

all about me.

Jess and I head back upstairs to

grab our shoes and purses and to

wait for the boys to

come pick us up.

I hear something slam

downstairs and I know

the fighting is about to start.

I rush Jess downstairs
and out of the house
before anyone starts yelling
or swearing.

Dave's dad drives up
in his green Range Rover
just as Jess and I walk
out the door.

The tight knot in my chest
unravels a bit
when I know
we're clear of the war zone.

For now,
my secret is safe.

THE CAR RIDE

Dave's dad drives
us from my house
to the school.

He's got pop music
playing on the radio,
trying to be cool.

So I hear you and Dave
are planning a bicycle trip?
he says to me.

I'm torn between excitement
that Dave told his dad
about our plans
and worry that he's getting
too attached to me too quickly.

I know I'll just disappoint him.
Or that he'll find out about my parents
and then he'll run away.

Oh, well, we haven't really made
any big plans,
I say, downplaying how excited
I actually am.

Dave's smile falters
for a moment.
Then he gets into talking
about possible routes,
and suddenly I'm close to forgetting
all about the fight
that must be raging back
at the house.

By the time we pull up

at the school,

I'm smiling again.

I've almost forgotten

about the anger at home.

Almost.

THE DANCE

In the school gym,
paper streamers and
bright balloons
are everywhere.

The music's fast
and couples are grinding
on each other.

Dave leads me over to
the drink table.
We get ourselves some punch,
then stand and chat.

The music changes to a super-oldie:
"Wonderful Tonight."

Dave takes my hand
and pulls me onto the dance floor.

He puts his hands on my waist.
I put my hands on his shoulders.
He pulls me closer, and we
start to sway slowly.

You seemed a little distracted
when you got into the car,
he says.
Is everything OK?

I nod my head and lie,
Everything's fine.

I wish he hadn't
brought it up.

I wish I couldn't feel

my own anger

bubbling up.

The song ends,

and we leave the dance floor

and find Jess and Sam

at a table.

Jess is talking about how

mad she is that she only got

93% on her English paper.

Don't feel bad about that,

Dave says.

She won't give me anything

over 90% on any of my papers.

How about you, Anna?

He turns to me.

I slump back in my chair
because my grades are worse
than any of theirs.
Especially this year.

I don't wanna talk
about it,
I say.
I really don't need Dave
to think I'm stupid,
like my dad does.

Oh, don't be embarrassed,
Jess says.
They're just grades.

I feel the anger
rising in my stomach,
turning my cheeks red,
and I refuse

to lose control here,

tonight.

I said I don't want
to talk about it,
I snap, standing up.

I know I'm being dramatic,
but I grab my purse
and speed walk toward
the doors.

Dave tries to follow me,
but I walk even faster,
and eventually he gives up.

And then I'm outside
and completely alone
again.

HOME AGAIN

I slip my heels off
and walk barefoot
through the grass
alongside the sidewalk,
all the way home.

The lights are all off
when I get to the house,
and Dad's car is gone.

I let myself in,
and head to the living
room to watch TV
and distract myself.

I turn the light on
and see Mom lying

across the couch,

out cold. There's a bottle of

whiskey on the table next to her.

Some fight they must've had.

I tap her on the shoulder.

Mom, wake up.

She justs moves a little

and then starts snoring.

I pause a moment,

take the bottle from the table,

and go upstairs.

THE BOTTLE

I sit on my bed, shaking.

I tilt the bottle back
and take a big gulp.
It burns my throat.

I almost spit it onto
my comforter.
But I force it down.

I've never had booze before.

I wait a moment,
then take another
big sip.

This time I
know what to expect.

It's not long

before the world

starts to slow

and I start to breathe

again.

With Mom asleep,

and Dad out of the house,

the anger seems to

slowly

disappear.

TRY TO REMEMBER

I try to remember
when we were
a happy family.
Actually happy, not just hiding
sadness and anger.

It wasn't that long ago.
Couldn't be more than a year...

Why can't I think of anything?

Maybe if I saw
some pictures.

I go up to the attic
where we keep
important things.

I bring two shoeboxes of photos
and the bottle down
to the living room.
I sit on the chair
opposite my drunk mother.

I almost hope
she'll wake up,
and see me with the bottle
of whiskey.

I almost hope
it gets me in trouble.

Maybe she'll wonder
why I'm drinking.

Maybe she'll realize
how much I'm hurting.

73

OLD PHOTOS

They must've loved each other
at some point, I tell myself.

I look through
old photos.

Me as a toddler
with two laughing parents
and our old dog, Bo,
under a Christmas tree.

The two of them
snuggled up on a couch at some
holiday party
before I was born.

The wedding photos—

Mom stuffing cake into
Dad's mouth.
Dad reaching out his hand
for the first dance.

They must've been happy.

I look up on the mantel,
to the photo of our last
family vacation.

Some beach in Maine.
Tan faces, tight smiles,
no light in their eyes.
I wonder when
they stopped.

I wonder why
they stopped.

I wonder why they

stay together

if all they do is fight.

I wonder if there's any point

at all to love

if this is where it ends up.

THE LETTERS

I assume the second shoebox

is full of more photos.

But instead I find

a stack of letters

from 20 years ago.

Mom's name in

Dad's handwriting

across the front.

I glance over at Mom,

snoring on the couch.

And then I pull the first

letter out of its envelope.

My Love,
it begins.
I can't wait to
see you again.

I read all the letters,
covering the year
between when they met
at a coffee shop
and when she moved
to be with him.

When they met,
he was in town
for a conference.
She was sitting in a coffee shop,
reading the newspaper
when he walked up.

They hit it off
as well as Dave and I had
at coffee the other day.

She lived here, in Buffalo,
and he lived in Atlanta.

He couldn't stop thinking
about her, but couldn't
drop everything and move
at that moment,
because he was still in school.
So they wrote
letters back and forth.

And visited each other
every time they could
get a long weekend.

He missed her.

She loved him.

Now they can't stand

each other.

It's like a math problem

I can't solve.

Suddenly I'm very tired.

I lean back in the chair

and close my eyes.

MORNING

I wake up feeling
like my brain is trying
to break out of my skull.

The photos are scattered around
the floor in front of me.

Mom is gone from
the couch.
The whiskey bottle
and letters are gone, too.

I get up,
gather the photos,
put them away.

I peek my head
into my parents' bedroom.
Mom is sound asleep.

The letters are around
her on the bed.

The bottle is empty
on the bedside table.

Dad is still gone.

The house is still quiet.

And I'm almost relieved.

IGNORE ALL

I plug my phone

in and wait for it

to power up.

After a minute, five messages

ding in all at once.

Three from Jess.

Where are you?

Are you OK?!?!?

PLEASE TEXT ME!!!!

Another two texts

from Dave.

Are you OK?

Do you want to

grab coffee tomorrow?

83

No.

I don't want to grab coffee.

I don't want to talk.

I want to be the person

who can hang out and not worry.

I want to be the person

who can chat happily about

travel and music.

If they find out

what a mess I am,

I'm worried they'll both

shrink away.

No one wants to be

around a miserable woman.

At least that's what
my dad says.

I ignore their texts
and turn off my phone.

DAD RETURNS

I'm scrolling through depressing news
on my phone and Mom's still
asleep upstairs
when Dad gets home
sometime after noon.

He has his briefcase and tells me
he's been at work.
He might have to go back in later.

I want to call him a liar,
tell him to stop
using work as an excuse.
I want to scream at him.
But I can't bring myself to yell.

So I ignore him.

A PARTY

I'm moping around
when Dave texts me
to see if I want to
go to a party tonight.

A party is perfect—
no one *really* talks
at a party. Harmless.

I text back to say I'll go,
just let me know when.

Luckily, Dad's left
for work again,
and Mom's upstairs, passed out again.

They can't tell me what to do

or who to be

or how to feel

if I'm not around.

In the dining room,

I open the cupboard

and pull out a bottle

of vodka to bring

to the party.

I know they'll notice

it's gone.

Right now, I don't care.

I close the door quietly

and grab my bike

from the back.

When I come down the driveway,

Jess and Sam and Dave are out front

on their bikes, ready to go.

It's not far to the party.

We drop our bikes in the backyard

and walk into the house.

As I guessed,

the music's too loud,

and I can't hear anything

anyone says to me.

Jess and I walk into

the kitchen to find some soda

to mix with the vodka.

I pour a lot of booze

into my cup before

I add the soda.

And then we head
into the party
to find our dates
and mingle a bit.

I let Dave put his arm
around my waist.
I lean my head
into his shoulder
as we chat
with some of his friends
from the baseball team.

I don't know how many
drinks I've had before
I start feeling nauseous and tired.
Dave hasn't been drinking as much
and he notices
I'm not feeling good.

He leads me into the kitchen
and finds some food
and a glass of water.
You wanna head home?

I nod. I'm not sure
how good I'll be on the bike,
but I just want my bed.

I get on my bike
and steady myself.
Then I wobble
and almost fall over.
Dave catches me.

OK, he says.
Let me just walk you home.
I think that'll be safer.

We grab our bikes
and push them up the street.

TROUBLE

Halfway home I stop

to throw up

by the side of the street.

Dave stands behind me,

rubbing my back.

And then there are

flashing lights behind us.

Cops asking us questions

and saying how we reek of alcohol.

And they look at our learner's permits

and get our addresses.

And I'm too drunk to really know

what's going on

except that it's not good.

And suddenly I'm in the back
of one of the cop cars,
on a hard plastic seat.
And my jeans are covered in vomit.
And I'm cold.
I look out the window
and see Dave being pushed
into another cop car.

It doesn't take long
for them to drive me
to my house.

They go up to the door
and ring the bell.
Mom answers the door.
She looks startled,
and then angry.

After a few minutes,

they collect me from the car

and hand me over

to my mom.

She starts yelling as soon

as we're in the house

and the door is closed.

What were you thinking?

she yells.

This isn't like you. You don't pull

this kind of stuff. And you know

what? They're fining you fifty dollars.

Are you listening to me?

I'm not really listening.

I'm feeling worse

by the second.

The room is spinning,

and I think I'm gonna be sick

again.

And I just hope that Dave is OK.

He must hate me now.

I fall asleep on the couch,

thinking about how I've already

screwed everything up

between us.

I WAKE UP

on the couch.

Mom and Dad sit across

from me in separate chairs.

I'm in for the lecture

of my life.

For the first time

in almost a year,

they're a united front.

Did that Dave kid pressure you

to drink?

Dad asks.

I shake my head no.

Then I feel dizzy.

I miss a lot of what

they say,

but I tune back in

for the end.

Dad says,

No more going out

until after vacation.

You can study at Jess's,

as long as her parents are there.

But no more Dave. You two are done.

That last bit hurts the most.

Later,

I text Dave to make sure

he's OK.

Yeah, but I'm grounded,

he says.

Me too,

I say.

And I'm sorry.

Don't be sorry.
It's as much my fault
as yours. See you at school?

Well, at least he doesn't hate me.

Yet.

STUDY PLANS

I make plans to study
with Jess. It's the only way
my parents will let me
out of the house.

Finals start in a couple of weeks.

But we have papers due
this week that need work.

I've been so worried about
my parents and about
my friends finding out
about my parents
that I've been putting off
my schoolwork.

Instead of studying,
I've been overthinking
and listening to music
and watching reality TV
shows about hoarders
and celebrity housewives.

My grades have slipped
lower than they've ever been.

Finals are my last chance
to pull my grades
back up and prove
to my Dad that I'm smart.

To prove to myself
that someday I might get out
of this place.

APPARENTLY

By the time I get up,

Mom and Dad

are back to yelling.

Apparently he left a bunch

of dirty dishes in the sink.

And apparently

Mom has been

drinking all day.

Apparently

he called her a drunk

and blamed my behavior

on her.

And apparently

she called him a slob.

And apparently
they've been yelling
insults back
and forth
since midmorning.

Apparently
they don't care
that I'm hearing
all of this.

Apparently
their anger blinds them
to everything outside
of what they're feeling.

HEADPHONES IN

The only way

to not hear the shouting

is to put my headphones in

and turn the music

all the way up.

I've got a playlist

of all my angry music.

A mix of old-school Green Day and Nirvana

and then some Drake and Kanye.

It's the only thing

that drowns

out the sounds

coming from downstairs.

DISTRACTION

I write my final history paper
just to distract myself from my parents.
And from wanting to text Dave.

He keeps asking me for coffee
or a bike ride once we're not grounded.

I ignore him. What's the point anyway?
It's not like he likes me so much
he'd put up with my whole mess.
He's just being nice.

I'm halfway through my paper
on King Henry the Eighth
and all his wives.
And wondering if *that* family
has my family beat.

STRESS LESS

I spend every night
that week studying at Jess's.

Even though I'm
stressing about finals,
I feel myself
relax the longer I'm
away from home.

No one is shouting.
I can pay close attention
to what I'm studying.

Maybe this is how I'll feel
when I go away to college.
When I travel the world as a journalist.

Free from my parents
and their anger.

I feel bad for thinking that way,
but the thing is,
I'm sure my parents don't even
notice I'm gone.

It's no secret things are
getting worse.

Now Dad really only
comes home to sleep.
And Mom pretends she's
not drinking Jack Daniels
out of a coffee mug.

Jess asks if we can study
at my house tomorrow.
I change the subject.

FINALS

I hand in all my papers,

and then the tests begin.

Math formulas

and biology theories

and French vocab

run through my head

until finally

the week of the

tests arrives.

I think I messed

up a formula in geometry.

I know I mixed up

a couple words

in French.

I think I did OK

in biology.

And I know I did

pretty well in history.

The essay test in English

was a mess, but it will be

good enough.

I mean, I can't really

screw up much worse

than showing up at home drunk

in the back of a cop car.

Right?

HERE WE GO AGAIN

I know I should

be relieved

now that finals

are over.

But all I can think about

is that now I have to go

on vacation with

Mom and Dad.

NO ARGUMENTS

For some reason,

Mom and Dad have

decided that we'll

take our family vacation

in one car.

It'll bring us closer,

Mom says.

When I

open my mouth to respond,

she says,

No arguments, Anna.

No arguments? Does that apply

to you and Dad, too?

I say.

Yes, and that's enough

attitude from you,

she responds,

ending the conversation

on a lie.

IN THE CAR

It's 9:15 in the morning,
and Mom's still packing.

Dad and I have been ready
and sitting in the car
for half an hour.

Dad's muttering
under his breath.
He's fuming
when she's finally ready.

My headphones don't
quite drown out
the sound of
his backseat driving
or her road rage.

At least her anger

is focused

outside the car

for now.

But this is the first

hour of a eight-hour drive.

It's only a matter

of time before

she tells him to

shut up,

or he tells her

to calm down.

I wonder what it's like

to travel without

baggage.

PIT STOP

We pull off

at a highway rest stop

a couple hours

into the drive.

Dad rolls his eyes

when Mom gets

back into the car

with a big bag of

salt and vinegar chips

and a Hershey's bar.

He's driving now,

and she's snacking.

And I can see where the

next argument

will start.

Because he's about
to tell her she shouldn't
eat that.
And she's going to
ask if he's calling her
fat.
And he won't say
yes.
But he won't say
no, either.

And she'll demand
that he pull
off the highway
at the next exit,
no matter where
we are.
And we'll pull into a
parking lot somewhere,

and they'll get out

and scream at each other

until they can't

scream anymore.

And then they'll

get back in the car

and we'll drive off

like nothing's

happened.

And that's exactly

what happens.

If being a reporter doesn't

pan out,

maybe I can be a psychic?

As their voices

rise, so does my

blood pressure.

I can hear my heartbeat

in my ears

underneath my headphones.

I can't seem

to breathe.

I feel

the tightness grow

in my throat.

I squeeze my eyes shut tightly.

I will not let the tears fall.

FRESH AIR

I close my eyes so long
that I fall asleep
with my music
turned all the way up.

And then we're at the park.
The campsite is beautiful.
But cabin number six
is small. Just two twin beds
with hard vinyl mattresses.

There's a firepit
with benches around it.

We're surrounded by trees.

I rush off to explore
the woods and trails
around us before we
unpack the car.

I just want to drink in
the fresh air and run away
from my problems.

When I am deep
in the woods,
I slip my shoes off,
wiggle my toes,
and feel the soft
soil beneath my feet.

And for the first time
in a long time,
I feel okay.

THE PATH

The path I take leads up a small hill
and then down toward a lake.

I stand at the edge
of the water and look around.

It's early afternoon
and getting pretty hot.

At the opposite shore of the lake,
there's a crowded public beach.

I walk along
the quiet side
of the lake.

The water is cool
and soft on my bare feet.

I'm so happy

to be outside that I lose track

of how far I've walked.

And suddenly I'm walking onto

the public beach,

which is full of happy families

and groups of teenagers

playing Frisbee

and eating picnic lunches.

I wander over

to an empty picnic table

and soak up sun

and watch everyone

having fun.

NEW FRIENDS

I'm sitting there
enjoying the weather
when a Frisbee whizzes
past my head.

A teenage girl
almost trips over the table
as she goes after the Frisbee.
She's very tall and thin,
with light brown hair
tied up in a long ponytail.

Oh my gosh, I'm so sorry!
she says to me.
*Hey, do you want
to play with us?*

I shake my head no.

But she insists. Then she's
telling me everyone's names.

She's Shaye, and there's
her girlfriend Mackenzie,
her brother Patrick,
and their friend Tyler.
Pat is taller and thinner
than Shaye, which I didn't
think was possible.
He's got shaggy brown hair.

We throw the Frisbee
around for awhile longer,
even though I have terrible aim.
Then we hang out on
a big tie-dye beach blanket,
chatting for awhile.

They're from Ohio,
and they're here with Shaye
and Pat's mother.
While the others are talking
about something from back home,
Pat turns to talk to me.

So earlier you said something
about wanting to travel
for a living.
Have you been anywhere super cool?

I'm surprised that he
was even listening.

Nowhere cool yet,
I say.
But I really want to see every bit
of the world and meet important people
and report on important things.

Things that matter, you know?
I smile, thinking about the future.

Of what could be.

Patrick says,
I've always wanted to just
road-trip across the country.
I guess that's not quite as
exciting as covering
breaking news in the Middle East
or anything, though.

As long as it's an adventure,
I say, and he smiles.

When it's time to
leave the beach,
Shaye tells me they're staying

in cabin number four,

and they invite me to dinner.

I tell them I'll have to ask

my parents first,

but I'll stop by

if I can.

CAMPFIRE

I walk back
around the lake
to our cabin.

I return just as Mom
is setting up the campfire.

Dad is nowhere
to be found.

I tell Mom
about the invitation.
She frowns and says,
Well, why don't you invite your
friends to our campfire?
I have hot dogs
and marshmallows.

She doesn't want
to be alone at the campfire,
while Dad and I have
better things to do.

I tell her I'll run over
and ask them.

And when they say yes,
I feel that familiar
sense of dread.

SUNSET

Mom and I are
sitting by the lake,
watching the sun
go down over
the water,
when we hear
the car pull up.

Dad's back at last.

Mom mutters something
under her breath,
but I can't quite hear it.
I'm not sure I want to
hear it.

Dad gets out and explains
that he had to make a call
back to the office,
but now he should be
free for the rest
of the week.

Mom rolls her eyes,
doesn't believe him
for a second.

She grabs a lighter
and flicks it on
under the newspapers.

She squats by the firepit,
poking at it
until the big logs catch fire.

POLITE ANGER

I hear Shaye's
voice talking loudly
from the main road.
Just as the flames are starting
to dance high into the air.

I'm nervous to have them over
now that Dad's back.

But it's too late
to backtrack now.
They come around the corner,
each carrying a bag
full of camping snacks.
Mom and Dad
are both polite
as they greet
my friends.

Sometimes they're able
to keep it together.

We all sit around
the fire.
I see Mom and Dad
glare at each other
a couple times.
But they keep their mouths shut.

Luckily, Pat is telling a funny story.

He's telling us about how
when he was 12, he decided to
hitchhike to Cleveland.
And how Shaye, who was 14,
tried to stop him, but got roped into the plan.

They both got busted. But Pat got
a Rock and Roll Hall of Fame keychain.
And that's all that matters!

I realize I'm a little jealous of him

because he's the sort

of person who seems to

jump into something without

worrying about every bad thing

that might happen.

Pat is jumping around.

He's doing funny voices,

and pausing just

at the right moment.

Despite my best efforts,

I crack up at his antics.

We all laugh and laugh.

COMFORTABLE

We stay up late. We
hang around the fire
long after my parents
have gone to bed.

The air has gotten cold.
But we have the fire
and hot chocolate.
We are warm
and laughing.

After a while we start
playing truth or dare.

Tyler chooses dare and eats a spider.

Pat goes and chooses dare, too.

Mackenzie dares him to stand up

on the bench and sing

the worst song he can think of.

He sings some '80s pop song.

He takes a proud bow before sitting back down.

Then it's my turn.

I choose truth, because honestly,

I'm afraid I'm going to have to sing

or eat a bug.

OK,

Pat says.

How old were you

when you had your first kiss?

I stop cold at that.

Think for a moment

about whether I should tell

the truth, or make up a lie.

Truth is,
I say.
I haven't had my first kiss yet.

I stare at the ground,
worried that they're
judging me terribly.
Until Mackenzie speaks up.

My first kiss was with Shaye,
she says, smiling.
And that was just
like a month ago.

They all start talking
about their first kisses,
and first dates, and
then we're all laughing again.
I finally feel comfortable.
I've completely forgotten how
embarrassed I felt.

When they leave,

it's two in the morning.

I make sure the fire

is out. And then I slip into

my sleeping bag.

I'm still smiling as I

fall asleep.

WAKING UP

I wake up to the smell
of the camp stove outside.
And to the sound of my parents
yelling again.

It's the same
words as always.

He calls her
miserable and mean.

She calls him a loser,
tells him to stop working
all the time and have a life
for once.

I don't know how they can
keep having this argument
over and
over and
over again.

I don't know how *I* can
keep *hearing* this argument
over and
over and
over again.

Did you just shove me?
he yells, surprised.

Yeah, well you wouldn't
get out of my way,
she snaps.

I hear a clattering,
something falling over.

139

And now *I'm* angry.

I'M ANGRY

that this has

been my life

for so long now.

I'm angry

that I hate my home

so much that I

look for ways to

run away.

And finally,

I'm angry

that it can't always

be like last night,

when they at least

pretended.

BOILING OVER

I rush out of the cabin

and see the camp stove

tipped over. Cooking

supplies scattered all over.

Mom's holding the knife

she'd been using to slice an apple.

I can see how tightly

she's gripping it in her anger.

I'm scared,

but I'm also still angry,

and the anger makes me

brave and stupid.

And finally I say the words

out loud, and to their faces.

SNAP

Why don't you
guys just break up?

I say. My hands shake.

They stop their yelling
and turn to stare at me.

Excuse me?
Mom asks, taking a breath
and carefully setting the knife
down on the picnic table.

Dad is too shocked
to say anything.

I shake my head.

You drive each other
crazy, and not in the good way.
I mean, jeez, Mom,
you looked like you
were ready to gut Dad
with that knife.

I pause and take a breath.
I'm still really freaked out
about the knife.

I knew they hated each other
but I never thought it would
get that bad.

And guess what?
You drive me crazy, too.
You think it's easy,
having you guys shouting
and fighting all the time?

My voice is shaking,

and I wish I could stop that,

but I keep speaking anyway.

You think it doesn't hurt

me when you guys try

to use me against

each other?

Honestly, we'd all

be happier if you two

split up.

I storm past them

and into the woods,

before either of them

can say anything.

TEARS

When I stop
running, I'm halfway
to the public beach.

I sit down on a large rock
by the edge of the lake.

Staring into the water,
I finally let my tears
fall.

The tears I refused to shed
all those nights before,
and at the dance,
and in the car.

And I let myself feel

my anger and sadness

instead of focusing

on my parents,

and pretending

my feelings

aren't important.

I realize then that I've let fear

overrule every other emotion

for a long time.

I've let it ruin happiness.

I've let it silence me

when I should've spoken up.

WHAT'S WRONG?

The tears are still drying
on my cheeks when I hear
footsteps splashing
through the water.

I look up and see that Pat
is walking toward me.

I thought that was you
I saw across the water,
he says as he approaches.

I try to smile
at him, but fail
as the tears start falling
again.

Oh, hey, what's wrong?
he asks. He comes closer
to hug me, even though we
just met.

It's nothing,
I say.
He steps back and I can see
he doesn't believe me.

I know you
don't really know
me,
he says.
But I can see
how upset you are.
It's your parents, isn't it?

149

SPLIT

How did you know?
I ask,

wiping the tears from my eyes.

He pauses for a moment,
thinking carefully
about what to say.

Me and Shaye, our parents split
up a couple years ago,
he says.
I know what it's like to have
friends over when you're
afraid of what your parents
will say or do to each other.

Really?

I ask.

Really, Anna,

he says.

I get it.

Then I let him

put an arm around me

and I don't feel so alone.

TRUST

We sit there, arms wrapped
around each other for a while.

Me and this stranger.

When we pull apart I can see
he has tears in his eyes, too.
Before, I'd only met the happy,
goofball version of Pat.

I'm surprised by this serious,
sincere attitude.

Can I tell you something?
Pat asks.

Of course,
I say, sniffling a bit.

He speaks very
slowly,
choosing
his words.

I know this
sounds awful,
but things got
a lot better after
Mom and Dad split.
Yeah, they still make
rude comments
about each other.
But I haven't
heard either of them
yell like they used to
in almost a year.

I think to myself
about how I couldn't
bring myself to
talk to my closest
friend about this.

And I think
about how
hard it must be
for him to tell a
girl he's just met.

I nod
and look him
in the eye.

I told them
to break up today,
I say,
feeling guilty.

It will be OK, alright?
he says.
It won't be
easy, always.
But it will be OK.

We lock eyes.

And we're so close.

And I trust him

right now

more than I've

trusted anyone

in a long time.

And then his lips are on mine,

and it's my first kiss.

FOR A MOMENT

I forget to worry

about everything

wrong in my life.

MOVING FORWARD

The car is gone when I go back
to the cabin to face my parents.

I go inside
and see that Mom
is lying facedown
on her bed. She's sobbing,
clutching her pillow.

Mom? I'm sorry
if what I said hurt you,
I say as I kneel
beside her bed.

She turns her head
to look at me.
Her face is red and puffy.

It's OK, honey,
she says.
Maybe it needed to be said.

She sits up on her bed.

Your father and I,
we've been holding onto
the marriage. Trying to deny
how bad it's gotten.

She hugs me, for the
first time in a long time.
Seems to be
happening a lot
today.

After we get home
from vacation,

your father and I
will talk more
about what
we're going to do.

I feel a little better,
knowing that this is out
in the open.

That they're handling it.
That I don't have to.

Um, where is Dad?
I ask.

He went
to book a flight
back home for tomorrow
morning.

Mom's quiet

for a moment.

Honey, I know

this is gonna be

hard. But maybe you're

right—maybe it's the right thing.

FREE

Mom falls asleep,

and I slip into

my bathing suit

and head down

to the little beach

near our cabin.

I swim a lap across to

the other beach

and back.

I feel good.

I feel *free*.

I swim back

across.

Shaye and Pat

and the others are back at

the beach.

I get out of the water.

Pat gives me

a hug, and

asks me how

I'm feeling.

This is the first

time in my life

that I am sure a boy likes me

as much as I like him.

And I realize now

that maybe back home,

Dave wasn't just being nice.

Maybe he really liked me, too.

And I realize how poorly I treated him.

I know that after vacation,

Pat and I won't be a couple,

although I hope we stay in touch.

But I think that when I get home,

I'll have to give Dave a real chance.

And an apology.

And maybe it'll be worth it.

To let someone in.

To let him know me

in my best moments

and in my messiest ones.

GOODBYE

Now that Pat knows my
worst secret, it's easy
to feel like myself around him.
It's so good to be around
new friends who *know*.
I've almost forgotten
that in another four days,
I'll be going back home.

As it turns out,
they're leaving tomorrow.
Pat looks sad when he tells me.

But he gives me
his phone number.

He tells me to text him.

Especially when things get difficult
between my parents.

Whatever happens when
you get home, remember
you've got a friend out there.

The five of us spend the rest
of the day like we spent
that first day.

We play Frisbee, swim,
and hang out on the beach.

That night I go to their
campfire and we all
tell ghost stories
and eat too many
marshmallows.

They all hug me,

and promise

to stay in touch.

DAD'S STORY

When I get back to the cabin,
Dad's back
and still awake.

He's sitting at our firepit,
staring into the flames.

Dad? Are you OK?
I ask.

I've had better days,
he says.

I sit down next to him
on the bench, and put my
arm around his shoulder.

I'm sorry
for what I said,
I tell him.

Anna, I think I'm the one
who should say sorry to you.

I keep my eyes
on the fire.
If I look at him I think I might
cry again.

I'm sorry for ignoring you,
he says.
I'm sorry
for being self-centered.
And I'm sorry
that I didn't notice
how all the yelling
was hurting you.

I guess...
I'm sorry I didn't listen.

I nod, and accept his apology.
I know it's not fair,
but I blame Mom more.

I blame her for her drinking.
For letting her drinking
get so out of hand
that she lost her job.

And I blame her for
being so bitter about
losing her job
that she resented Dad's success.

But Dad could be cruel, too.
And it takes two sides to start a war.

IT WILL BE OK

I wake up early
the next morning
to say goodbye to Dad
before he leaves.

I'm so sorry, honey.
I love you,
he says
again and again.
I think he might cry.

It's OK, Dad.
It's going to be OK,
I say, echoing Pat's words
until I almost believe them.

It feels weird to me
to be saying these words

to someone who's said them to me

so many times

over skinned-knee-

falls off my bicycle.

I wave from the campsite

as Mom drives Dad

off to the airport.

She'll be back in a few hours.

For now I have the cabin,

the woods, and the lake

to myself.

ALONE

While Mom's gone
I sit by the lakeside
and think about
the past few months.
And about what Pat said.

I wonder if it all would've
been easier
if I'd had a brother or sister
to talk to.

I think about all the time
I spent alone,
trying not to cry,
and whether it would've been
different to have someone
else around.

I'm not sure.

For all I know,

my imaginary sibling

would've gotten into

as much trouble

as me. Or gotten me

into worse trouble.

I guess Jess is the closest

thing I have to a sister.

She would've been the one

trying to hitchhike

when she was 12.

And I probably would've

followed her.

We would have told

each other everything,

and I wouldn't have

had to hide my problems.

And then I realize

I never had to hide

a thing from her.

She gave me every opportunity

to open up

and to tell her what was going on.

And I didn't.

I just pushed her away.

I just pushed everyone away.

MOM'S STORY

When Mom gets back,
she wants to talk.

We stuff a backpack
with snacks and water
and go on a hike.

She listens to me
when I tell her about how
hard it's been hearing
the fights and hiding them
from my friends.

She seems like she didn't
realize before how hard it
was on me.

175

Which maybe makes it worse.

But at least she knows now.

She tells me how sorry she is.

And then she tells me

her side.

She tells me about how Dad's

long hours at work chipped away

at their relationship.

How often she ended up

drinking alone

after I'd gone to bed.

And how she always wanted

to feel like a real family

who spends time together.

I think back to before Dad worked

all the time.

Before Mom was always drunk.

A camping trip
when I was maybe 10.

So many of the details
are the same as this trip—
the campfires, the marshmallows,
the lake, and the outdoors.
And I wonder if Mom was trying
to recapture that vacation
and that feeling.

She was trying
to go back in time.

I'm happy
to listen to her.

But I also know that Dad
isn't all to blame.
And I kind of feel like
she's not actually apologizing.
Like she's just making excuses.

Because she's still mad,
and she blames him
for everything.

And maybe that's what she needs
to feel right now.
But at some point she has to
realize that she screwed up, too.

DON'T OVERTHINK

The next few days
fly by. Mom and I
spend our days swimming
and hiking and doing
everything we can
to not think too much.

I'm almost
happy
to go home
when we start
packing the car
up.

HONESTY

We leave the campsite
early in the morning.

I stare out the car window,
thinking about what a week
it's been.

I never expected
to find new friends,
have my first kiss,
or be so honest
with my parents.

I never expected
that I'd be brave enough
to tell my parents
the truth.

Now I have to
learn to be
honest with
the other people
in my life.

We stop at the first
coffee shop we see.
A little hole-in-the-wall place
with a colorful mural
on the back wall.

While we wait for our orders,
I take out my phone.
I have service for the first
time in a week.

Now it's time for me

to make sure

I keep in touch

with new friends.

And it's also time for me to fix

mistakes I've made

with old friends.

I text Pat:

Hey,

it's Anna,

how are things

in Ohio?

Next I text Dave:

Hey, I'm sorry

for ghosting you.

Can we get coffee when

I'm back in town?

Finally,

I text Jess:

You were right, I wasn't OK.

We should hang out soon.

I love you <3

COFFEE, AGAIN

Dave and I make plans

to hang out

a few days after I get home.

I'm sitting,

drinking my mocha,

when he walks into

the coffee shop.

My heart skips a beat

when I see him.

I think to myself

that this might be

more than a crush.

I've never allowed myself

to think that before.

He gets his order

and then sits down.

I'm glad you texted me,

he says, smiling.

I missed you,

and...I was worried about you.

I look him in the eye

and tell him,

I'm sorry

for blowing you off.

I was afraid you'd hate me.

I was so moody at the dance.

And such a drunken mess that other night.

I have a lot of baggage.

But...I like you a lot.

He grins even wider

when I tell him I like him.

I can feel my fear

melting into a smile.

Anna,

he says,

I don't think I could ever

hate you.

And somehow I believe that.

WANT TO KEEP READING?

If you liked this book, check out another book
from West 44 Books:

THE WICKED EDGE
BY NICOLE ELIZABETH

ISBN: 9781538382554

MOM GOT THE JOB FIRST

Smoholla Indian School
on the Colville Reservation
in Omak needed teachers. And
Amanda Robbins had a degree.

She started teaching
fourth grade
in the K-12 tribal school.
Drove across the river

from Okanogan,
where we lived
and I went to school,
to Omak every day.

SOON SHE MET THE BOYFRIEND

which seems like
the wrong word
for the 46-year-old guy
whose trailer we live in now.

Damon Adams is a tutor
in Smoholla's reading program.
I guess it's hard to resist a man
who teaches kids to sound out words.

They fell in love across
sight words and stories
or whatever. *It was his charm
and commitment*, Mom says.

*It was my muscles and
my dreamy Native eyes.*
Damon flexes. And then he
started showing up to everything.

SOCCER GAMES AND BIRTHDAY PARTIES

When he stuck his pull-up bar
in Mom's bedroom doorway,

I knew he was going to
be around for a while.

It bothered me and my brother at first.
Someone around who wasn't Dad.

But we knew
that Damon was a good guy.

Mom was
suddenly happy.

He brought her joy.
She teased him

about being a meathead.
And he pretended to get sad

until she gave him a kiss.
They're always talking

about the stars.

MOM AND DAD NEVER FIT TOGETHER

Something I couldn't
understand for a long time.

The divorce happened fast.
As a kid, it seemed very sudden.

A twisted, wide tree,
splitting in a lightning strike.

After four years,
it's still hard to let go.

Dad moved to the East Coast.
As far as he could get, it seemed.

And we stayed in Washington.
We get to visit in the summers,

but I miss him. How can your dad
be your dad over a phone?

After, Charlie left too. He graduated
high school the year before last.

Mom decided she and I needed
something fresh.

Walls without her old memories
stuck in the trim and the paint.

SO WE MOVED TO DAMON'S TRAILER

Charlie left for Seattle.
Making his way at University of Washington
with a loud girlfriend and
all of his Dave Matthews CDs.

He was gone and,
like Dad, I knew
he wouldn't come back.
Why would he?

I am getting used to it.

The trailer is small,
but I have my own room.
For Mom, it's a half hour
closer to Smoholla.

It's also out of
Okanogan school lines.
So my mother decided
I would come to school with her.

Check out more books at:
www.west44books.com

An imprint of Enslow Publishing

WEST **44** BOOKS™

ABOUT THE AUTHOR

Lexi Bruce is from Buffalo, New York, and received a degree in English and creative writing from Canisius College. She enjoys bicycling around her city and hiking whenever she can get out of the city. Lexi knows firsthand the toll divorce can take on a family, and on a young person hoping to find a healthy relationship. She wants this book to be a sign of hope for anyone who is going through this.